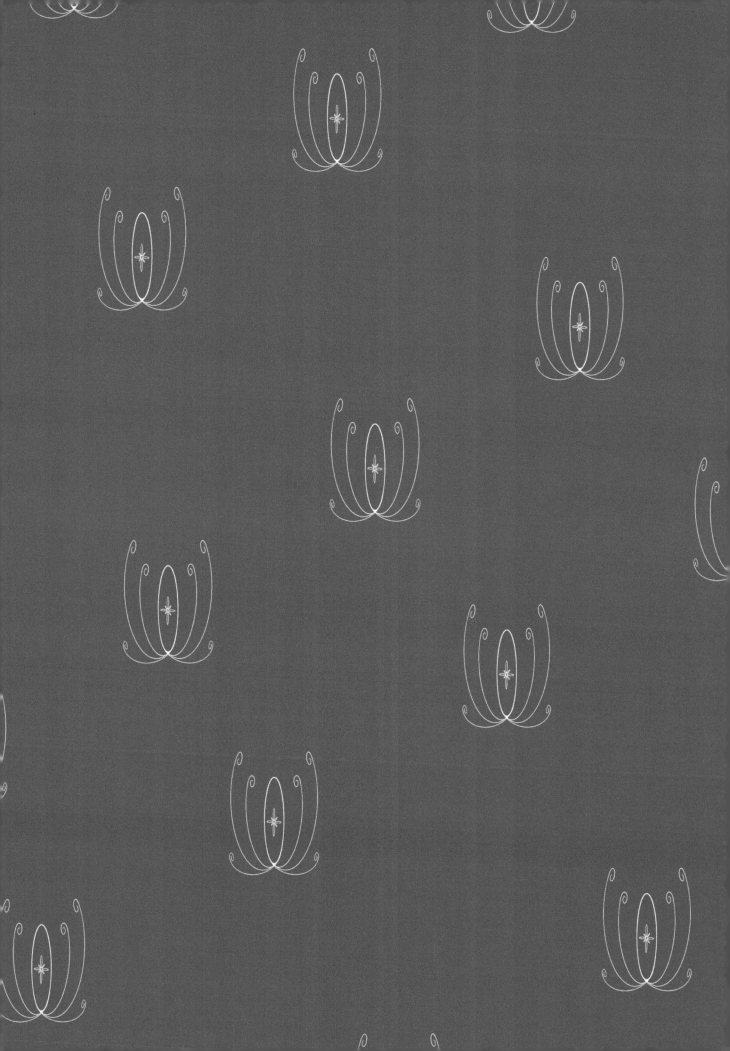

To my two biggest fans, my wife and mother:

Thank you for your support and love.

- Rick

To my wife and brother:

Thank you for your continual tolerance
and support. This book wouldn't be possible
without you.

- Matt

Goodnight Ship

Rick Martinez
Matt Pikarsky

Published by Rick Martinez
Auburn, NY 13201, USA

Library of Congress Control Number: 2021901641

ISBN 978-1-7329511-3-6

Printed in the United States of America

As I walk the decks of me ship, as a good Captain should,
Doing me rounds as quickly as I could.

I notice the moon is oh so full,
It makes the masts of the boat look so incredibly tall.

As I look up to the Crows Nest,
A good Pirate keeps watch over the sea,

I nod at him, and he waves back to me.

All is quiet and bright,
No need for lamps on this Summer's night.

As I head below deck to check on me crew,
I pass by the cook readying a big pot of tomorrow's stew.

It smelled so good, and I was willing and able,
When the cook offered me a taste in a bowl at the table.

With a smile on me face and a belly that's full,
Off to check on me buckos down the hall.

In the hold me crew fast asleep in their racks,
Snoring like bears,

"What the heck?"

Now up to the helmsman alone at the wheel,
Steering with barely a feel.

Keeping our course, with the wind at our backs,
And following the stars, he is me most trusted mate by far.

With a pat on his back and a smile on me face,
I know not to worry; he will get us to that place.

Off to me quarters, I go tired from a long day,
From sun up to sundown, don't you know?

As I open me door, the moon shines through me windows,
There are maps and charts strewn across me desk,
And a pile of gold and jewels glisten in the dark.

While me two black cats in a big leather chair,
Playing and making a mess
Right over there,

JUMP UP!

Right next to a half-full glass of rum.
Quickly I grab it and drink it down.

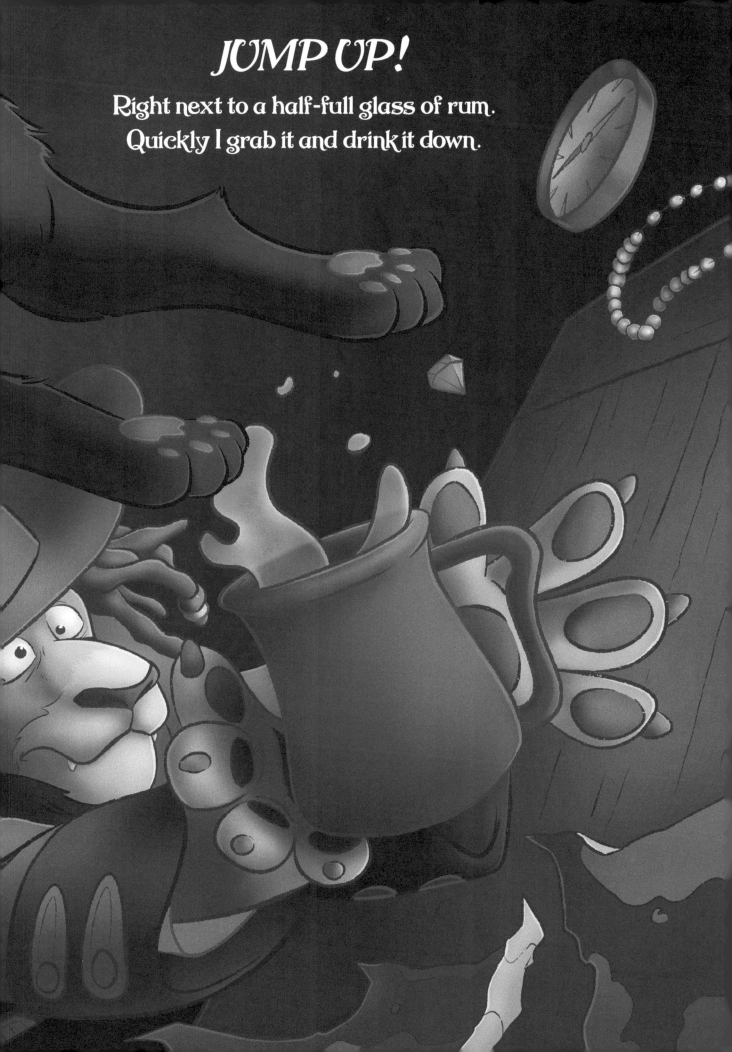

Now off to me bed, half-made and
Blankets all in a muss,
Right next to me fat parrot, Lush,
Who starts squawking,

HUSH!

Rocking with the waves, I don't have a care.
I kick off me boots and tussle me hair.
I toss me hat which knocks down a bat,
Which flies out me window just like that.

But before I lay me head to rest,
I recite these words for some luck at best:

Goodnight, ship,
Stay straight and true.

Goodnight, moon,
Light our way,
Keeping us safe from doom.

Goodnight, masts,
Hold those sails steadfast.

Goodnight, mate up in the nest,
Keep a weathered eye out for the rest.

Goodnight, cook,
You know what to do,
Making us enjoy every chew!

Goodnight, me crew,
Snoring like bears, rest well;
Ye worked hard from swabbing decks,
To hoisting sails.

Goodnight, helmsman, at the wheel,
Keep us straight and true to our prize,
That is oh, so real!

Goodnight, maps and charts,
Without you, I have no smarts.

Goodnight,
Me two black cats,
Making a mess,
Come to bed.
It's time to rest.

Goodnight, rum,
I'm glad I caught you,
before you were gone.

Goodnight, Lush, you big fat parrot,
Eat your cracker, and don't you say,
"HUSH!"

Goodnight, sea,
Thank you for what you have given me,
From me freedom to your sounds of tranquility,
Tis the only life for me.

Yo, Ho, Ho,
A Pirate, I Be!

Author Rick Martinez is a pirate afficionado and champion of children's literacy in his local community. He volunteers his time to libraries and schools, reading to children while dressed up in one of his many swashbuckling costumes.

Syracuse, NY native Matt Pikarsky has worked in freelance illustration for nearly 10 years, and has wanted to illustrate a children's book for just as long. He lives in his very cramped home with his wife, 3 children, 2 german shepherd mixes and a spastic cat.

CPSIA information can be obtained
at www.ICGtesting.com
Printed in the USA
LVHW071307050721
691872LV00001B/37